GOING
LOBSTERING

by Jerry Pallotta
Illustrated by Rob Bolster

Charlesbridge

For Mary T. Pallotta (Nana at the beach)

Published by
Charlesbridge Publishing
85 Main Street
Watertown, MA 02172
(617) 926-0329

Library of Congress
Catalog Card Number 90-080286
ISBN 0-88106-474-2 (softcover)
ISBN 0-88106-475-0 (hardcover)

Printed in the United States of America
(sc) 10   9   8   7   6   5   4   3   2   1
(hc) 10   9   8   7   6   5   4   3   2   1

It was a beautiful day at the beach. Linda and her little brother Erik were building sandcastles and looking for sea shells. When they looked out at the ocean, they saw a boat, and they wondered what the man in the boat was doing.

Their father came over and told them that the boat was a lobster boat and that the man in the boat was a lobsterman. A lobsterman uses traps to catch lobsters. After hearing all about lobsters and lobstering, Linda and Erik asked their father if they could go out on a lobster boat some day.

Their father decided to take them to the town pier to meet his old friend, Big Joe, the lobsterman. Their father told them that, if they were lucky, Big Joe would take them out lobstering to check some of his traps. Big Joe thought it was a fun idea.

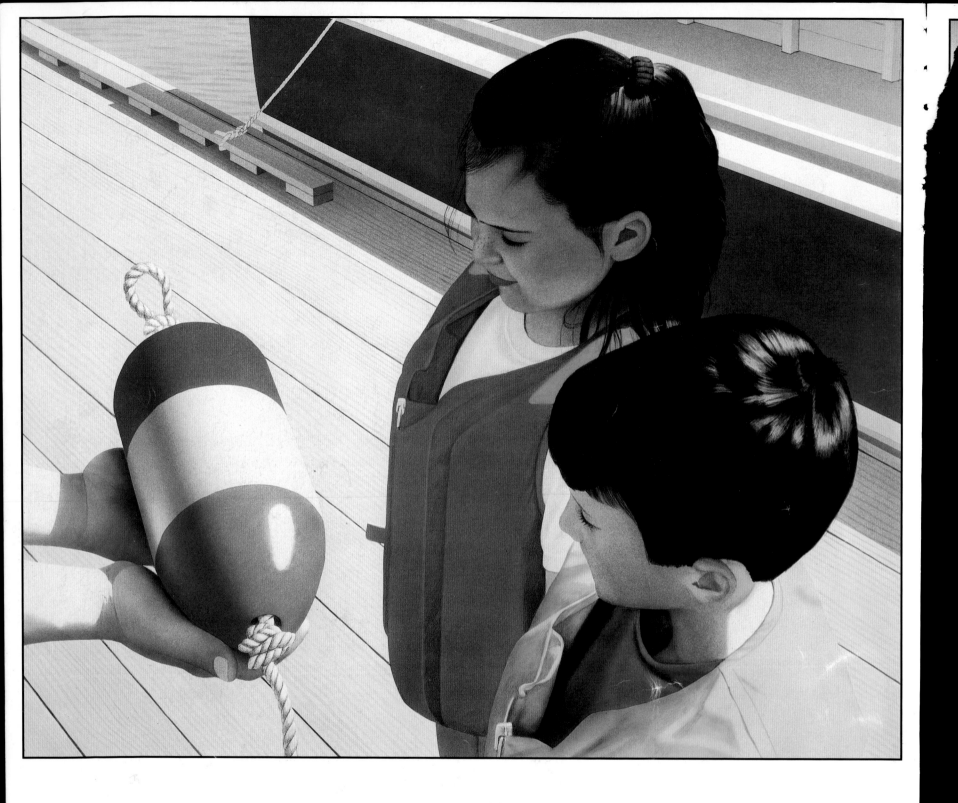

The first thing Big Joe did was to show Linda and Erik the buoys that float on top of the water and mark the location of his lobster traps. Big Joe's buoy colors were green, white, and red.

Their father decided to take them to the town pier to meet his old friend, Big Joe, the lobsterman. Their father told them that, if they were lucky, Big Joe would take them out lobstering to check some of his traps. Big Joe thought it was a fun idea.

The first thing Big Joe did was to show Linda and Erik the buoys that float on top of the water and mark the location of his lobster traps. Big Joe's buoy colors were green, white, and red.

As they left the harbor, Erik was hoping they would catch lots of lobsters. Big Joe told Linda and Erik to be on the lookout for his buoys.

Big Joe explained how a lobster trap works. The trap is baited with stinky dead fish. Then it is set on the bottom of the ocean. There is a rope attached to the trap so it can be pulled to the surface and checked for lobsters. A buoy marks the rope that is attached to the traps.

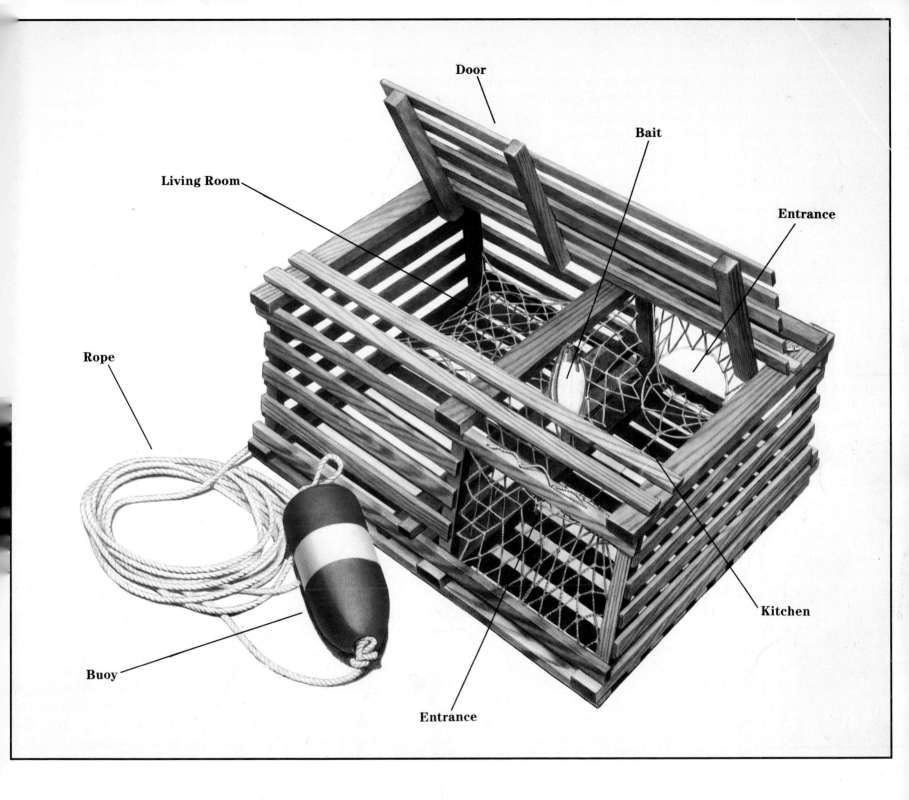

Door

Bait

Entrance

Living Room

Rope

Buoy

Kitchen

Entrance

Hungry lobsters are attracted by the smelly bait. There are openings in the sides of the trap so that the lobsters can climb in. Once the lobsters are inside the trap, it is difficult for them to get out.

Linda could not believe all the buoys she saw. Erik was amazed by all the different colors. Each lobsterman has his own colors, so he knows which buoys are his.

Linda was the first to find one of Big Joe's buoys. Erik remembered that the colors they were looking for were green, white, and red.

Big Joe grabbed his buoy. He put the rope through the pulley and wrapped it around the winch. He then began to pull up the first lobster trap. Linda and Erik were a little afraid. They did not know what to expect.

Unfortunately, the first trap did not have any lobsters in it, but it did have a flounder. Linda and Erik thought that this was a crazy lobster trap. It caught a fish instead of a lobster.

They pulled the second trap. It had two broken boards. Big Joe explained that they would have to fix the broken boards so that lobsters could not escape through the hole.

In the third lobster trap, they caught ten rock crabs but still no lobsters. Big Joe put bait on the bait hook, then threw all the crabs back into the ocean.

In the fourth lobster trap, they finally caught two lobsters. One lobster was much too small, but the other one looked big enough to keep.

Big Joe showed them the special gauge that a lobsterman uses to measure a lobster. A lobster is measured from its eye socket to the end of its back. The other lobster was also too small.

Before throwing the lobster back in, Big Joe showed Linda and Erik how to hold a lobster. The easiest way to pick it up is by its body with one hand. Then the lobster cannot bite you with its claw or hit you with its flapping tail.

In the fifth trap they caught a very big lobster. As he picked it up, Big Joe noticed that the very big lobster had thousands of lobster eggs on its tail. Lobsters with eggs have to be thrown back into the ocean.

Splash! Linda and Erik couldn't believe it! After finally catching a lobster big enough to keep, it still had to be thrown back. But it was the best thing to do. In the ocean the eggs will hatch, and thousands of baby lobsters will have a chance to grow. Linda wondered how the mother could possibly take care of so many baby lobsters.

When the sixth trap was pulled from the water, Linda and Erik were scared and almost started to cry. There was a shark in the trap! It took Big Joe a long time to get the shark out of the trap.

In the seventh lobster trap, they caught two lobsters that were big enough to keep. Now, finally, they had some they could take home to show their mother.

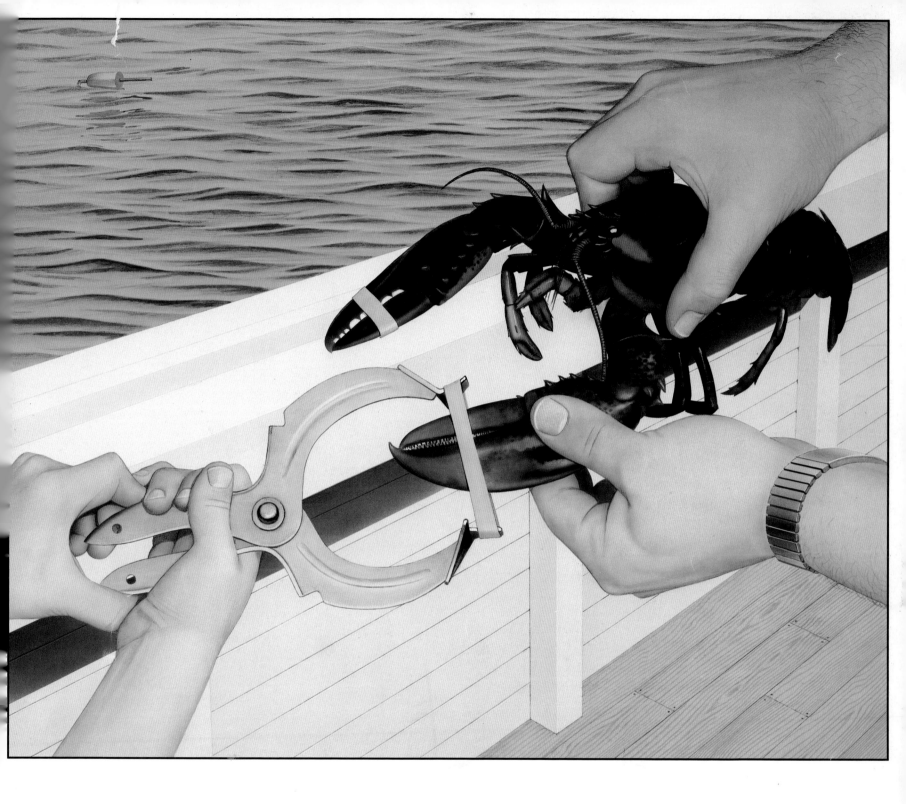

Big Joe helped Erik put rubber bands on the claws so that the lobsters could not bite anyone. Lobsters have two claws. One is a "cruncher claw" that is strong and dull. The other claw is a "scissors claw." It is sharp and quick.

Lobsters also have two antennas. They have eight legs. The first two legs on each side have little pinchers on them. They have tails that flap. One amazing thing about lobsters — when they lose an antenna, leg or claw, a new one grows back.

In the eighth lobster trap, they caught twenty-two crabs, six small lobsters, and four lobsters that were large enough to keep. Claws were snapping everywhere, and Big Joe had trouble pulling everything out without getting bit.

In the ninth lobster trap, no one could believe what happened. Big Joe was stunned. He had never caught a lobster this big. The lobster couldn't even get its cruncher claw into the opening of the trap.

They finally got it out. Wow! It was almost as big as Erik. This lobster was probably as big as the biggest one anyone has ever caught. Linda couldn't wait to tell all her friends about the gigantic lobster.

They pulled a few more traps. After they had caught ten lobsters that were large enough to keep, they steered the boat back toward the harbor.

After seeing how big lobsters can grow, Linda wanted to know what they eat. Big Joe told them that lobsters are scavengers. They eat anything they can. Snails, fish, periwinkles, mussels, clams, crabs and even other lobsters are just a few examples!

Erik wanted to know if lobsters eat hamburgers, fries, and pizza. Big Joe and Linda laughed. Big Joe told them to remember that lobsters eat anything. They would even eat pizza if they could find some.

Soon they were at the entrance of the harbor. Linda told Big Joe that going lobstering was really fun. Erik agreed.

They were back on the pier. Big Joe was happy because he had caught the biggest lobster he had ever seen. Linda was happy. Erik was happy. Now all of their friends want to go lobstering.